Steggie's Way

Written by June Counsel
Illustrated by Amanda Wood

Chapter 1

One bright Saturday morning, Clare, Ben and their little brother, Rob, went for a walk. They went across fields and over stiles and through a wood and down a lane until they came suddenly to a great big mess.

There were men in hard hats, diggers, JCBs, lorries and huge heaps of gravel and sand. There were holes and ruts and puddles and mud.

'It's the new road,' cried Clare, 'the new road they're building.'

'The hedges have gone!' gasped Ben.

'They've pulled them up,' explained Clare.

'The trees have gone,' cried Rob.

'They've bulldozed them flat,' said Ben.

'And our secret place? Where we made our den?' asked Rob, looking round.

'Gone,' said Ben. 'They've flattened everything.'

They walked sadly along by the edge of the mess until they came to a little pit. They stopped and stared. At the bottom was a *huge* EGG.

'Wow!' they all gasped.

'It's bigger than an ostrich egg,' said Ben.

'It's an elephant egg,' cried Rob.

'Don't be silly,' said Ben. 'Elephants don't lay eggs.'

5

Clare took off her sweater and laid it over the egg.

'Eggs have to be kept warm,' she said, 'or they don't hatch out. We'll take it home to Mum. She'll know what to do.' Their mum was the Headteacher of the village school.

Carefully they lifted the egg out of the pit and carried it away. The workmen never noticed. They were much too busy. The children carried it across the fields and over the stiles, stopping every now and then to put it down on the grass to have a rest.

When they got home they called out, 'Mum, Mum, come and see what we've found.'

'My goodness!' said their mum. 'Where did you find that?'

'By the new road,' they told her. 'Where they've pulled everything up and bulldozed everything down.'

'I've never seen an egg that big,'
said their mother. 'I wonder what
could be inside?'

So, on Monday morning, they
took the huge egg to school and
made a nest for it in the library
with cushions and newspaper.

They placed it near a radiator to
keep it warm. All the children in the
school came to look at the egg and
made guesses about what it might be.
'It could be a python's egg,' said a
boy. 'Or a turtle's egg,' said a girl.

Mrs Dear, the cleaner, joked, 'I
don't know what's in it, but it would
make a good breakfast for a family!'

In Assembly, Clare, Ben and Rob stood up and told the school how they found the egg. Then their mother held up a large red book.

'This will be OUR BOOK OF THE EGG,' she said. 'We'll write in it each day and record any changes in the egg.'

Where did the children find the egg?
What do you think is inside the egg?

Chapter 2

Every day the children looked at the egg. Every day they wrote in the book and every day all the writing said was NO CHANGE.

Then one day, just after home time, when Clare, Ben and Rob were standing by the egg waiting for their mum, something *did* happen. Clare heard something tapping.

'Listen!' cried Clare. 'Listen! Something's tapping *inside* the egg.'

They all stared at the egg. Suddenly, a crack ran across the top.

'Mum!' yelled Rob. 'Come quickly. The egg's opening!'

'Coming!' called Mum and came quickly out of her office.

The tapping got louder and louder, cracks were zigzagging all over the egg and bits of shell started falling off, and then, a scaly head on a scaly neck poked out! Two bright eyes looked at them and a mouthful of teeth went SNAP! SNAP! SNAP!

'Children,' cried their mum coming in, 'move back a bit. Don't be afraid. It's only a baby and there are four of us and only one of it.'

'It's a dinosaur,' said Clare.

'It's a Tyrannosaurus rex!' squealed Rob, clutching his mum's hand.

A humpy back came out of the broken egg. It had two rows of knobs on it and a long tail with four spikes on the end.

'No, it's a Stegosaurus,' laughed Clare.

'Good,' grinned Ben. 'Then it won't eat us. Stegosaurus was a plant eater.'

Just then Mrs Dear came in. 'Wow!' she gasped. 'That is some hen!'

'It's a Stegosaurus!' they told her.

'Is it?' she said. 'Well, welcome Steggie. My, what a mess you've made.'

The next day each class in turn saw Steggie. They oohed and aahed at the little dinosaur in her nest. After school all the children's parents lined up to see her and they oohed and aahed. In the evening, the school governors came to see her. They oohed and aahed too, and they held a meeting to decide what to do about her.

'We must keep her!' they said. 'We'll be the only school to have a living dinosaur as a pet.'

Chapter 3

So Steggie stayed. A large wooden box padded with newspaper was made for her, and everyday someone brought fresh food for her – grass, lettuce, cabbage and apples.

'It's surprising how fast she's growing,' said Ben. 'I didn't know dinosaurs grew that fast.'

'Our grass and vegetables are probably juicier than the ones the dinosaurs had,' said Clare.

'And she doesn't have to share with other dinosaurs,' said Rob, who was always being told to share.

'Well,' decided their mum, 'if she grows much bigger, I think she'll have to go in the playground.'

'Hooray!' cheered the children. 'Then we can have rides on her.'

So they put Steggie in the playground and they did have rides on her. It was great fun, but it was not really suitable. Steggie giving rides didn't leave much room for skipping and hopscotch and chasing.

'Put her in the swimming pool,' said Mrs Dear. 'She'd love that.'

Steggie did! But when she got in – SPLASH! All the water came out.

'Oh dear,' sighed the Headteacher, and after school, she went across the field to a friendly farmer.

'She can go in Long Meadow,' said the farmer. 'That's next to the school, so the children will still see her.'

So Steggie went into Long Meadow. The sheep didn't mind, but the cows did. A few days later, the farmer came to see the Headteacher.

'I'm really sorry,' he said, 'but my cows aren't giving any milk. It's Steggie. They just don't want her in their field.'

'Well now,' said the Headteacher to her governors that evening. 'What are we to do with Steggie?'

17

The governors thought and thought, then one said, 'What about Flowery Meadows? There's masses of space and no cows!'

Flowery Meadows was a country park. It had a river, a lake, islands, picnic places and tracks for jogging, cycling and horse riding. So early on Sunday morning, Ben, Clare, Rob and Mum got on their bikes and took Steggie to Flowery Meadows.

'Delighted to have her,' said the Manager. 'We'll be the only country park to have a living dinosaur.'

Steggie *was* happy. Her food was brought in specially, so she didn't eat all the grass in the meadows. But she went on growing *and* she began to explore, and it wasn't long before people started complaining to the Manager.

Windsurfers said she made waves on the lake and upset them. Joggers said they had to jump over her tail, or run under her. Riders said she startled the horses.

The Manager rang the Headteacher and the Headteacher rang her governors.

'Steggie will have to leave the park,' she told them. 'But where can she go?'

One of the governors said, 'Let me write to my brother, the Mayor. He knows lots of important people.'

So he did and the Mayor wrote to dozens of important people, but none of them wanted a Stegosaurus that was still growing.

Then, one day, a letter came.

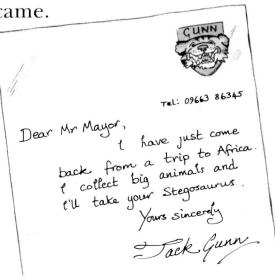

Tel: 09663 86345

Dear Mr Mayor,
    I have just come back from a trip to Africa. I collect big animals and I'll take your Stegosaurus.
        Yours sincerely
            Jack Gunn

The Mayor dialled the number on the letter. A man with a big booming voice answered the phone.

'Jack Gunn speaking.'

'Mr Gunn,' said the Mayor. 'I've just read your letter offering to take Steggie. The Headteacher will be delighted, but, are you sure you have enough room? Steggie is still growing.'

A huge laugh came down the phone. 'Quite sure, Mr Mayor. I like large animals. I'll have a special lorry built to transport Steggie and send it down for her.'

At once the Mayor phoned the Headteacher. 'I can't say I liked the sound of Mr Gunn, but he likes large animals and he wants Steggie.'

'Then we must accept his offer,' said the Headteacher. 'I will tell the children.'

The next day at Assembly, she spoke to the children.

'The Mayor has found someone to take care of Steggie. She will be going a long way from us, which is sad, but she will have a home and all the space she needs, because Steggie has a lot more growing to do!'

Why couldn't Steggie stay in the school?

What was wrong with the other places they tried?

Do you think Steggie will be happy with Mr Gunn?

Chapter 4

Mr Gunn had a lorry built with a powerful engine and a long trailer. He had Steggie's favourite foods, cabbage, apples, cucumbers, piled up at one end of the trailer. Then he hired a driver and his mate to drive to Flowery Meadows, the country park.

'Now, boys,' he said. 'Drive through the night. Get there early in the morning before anyone's about. Here's five hundred pounds each *and* there'll be another five hundred when you bring Steggie back.'

He waved them off and they drove through the night.

They reached Flowery Meadows just as the sun was rising. They found Steggie in one of the meadows, but she was not alone. Clare, Ben and Rob had come to say goodbye to her.

'Kids!' groaned the driver. 'Bloomin' kids!'

'They're blubbing,' added his mate. 'What'll we do?'

'Leave it to me,' said the driver. 'I've got kids of my own.'

They walked towards the children. Clare was sniffling and patting Steggie's leg. Ben was rubbing his eyes and stroking Steggie's nose. Rob was just bawling.

'Now then, what are you kids doing out here without your Ma?' asked the driver.

'Sh-she s-said we could c-come t-to say g-goodbye to Steggie,' sniffed Clare.

'S-Steggie's our f-friend!' added Ben.

'Steggie's OURS! We found the EGG!' roared Rob.

'Is that so?' said the driver. 'Now just you tell me all about it.'

Sniffing and sobbing, the children told him how they'd found the huge egg and rescued it from being crushed, how they'd looked after it, how Steggie had lived in their school and how *everyone* loved her.

Steggie, meanwhile, had seen the apples and cucumbers piled up on the trailer and was making her way towards it. The driver and his mate turned to follow her.

'See kids, she's looking forward
to her little trip in the lorry.'

'Let's go and watch,' said Ben.

The children followed the men
and saw the driver press a button on
the trailer. The ramp came down and
Steggie moved up on to it. She found
the pile of green stuff and began to
eat. The driver pressed the button
again and the ramp came up again.
Then he and his mate pulled a
strong canvas hood over the trailer
to hide Steggie. They could still hear
her though, crunching and champing.

'There, listen to that,' said the mate, 'she's happy.'

'We have to go,' Clare said, sadly. 'Something very important is happening and we have to be at school early. Come on, Rob.'

But Rob wouldn't go.

'Will the man be kind to Steggie?' he asked, looking up at the driver.

The driver grinned. 'Kind? He loves animals, can't get enough of them.' He winked at his mate. 'Got them everywhere – in his house, on his walls. Walks on them, sits on them. Why, there's a grizzly bear, eight foot tall, in the hall, with its mouth open in a grin and its arms out ready to hug you when you come in.'

'Come *on*, Rob,' cried Clare, dragging him away. 'We'll be late.'

The three children set off at a run.

The mate turned to the driver. 'Now what? Straight back?'

The driver laughed. 'After driving all night? No, we park this trailer in a nice quiet spot, and have a kip, stretched out, on some nice soft grass.'

The mate looked worried. 'But what if people see the trailer?'

The driver snorted. 'Didn't you hear the kid? There's something on – school fete, probably. Everyone will be there.'

What do you think it means when it says, 'Mr Gunn sits and walks on his animals?'

Chapter 5

Rob, running along beside Clare said, 'That grizzly bear – in the man's hall – wouldn't he squash people when he hugged them?'

'I expect he's trained not to,' gasped Clare.

'How-how do you – walk on animals? You can sit on them, but how-how do you walk on them?' panted Rob.

Ben said, 'You make them stand still first.'

'We'll look in books when we get home,' promised Clare, 'or ask Mum.'

'But Mum will be too busy,' said Ben.

'Then we'll ask Mrs Dear. She knows lots of things,' Clare said, as they panted up to the school gate.

Their mum was helping the other children on to the school bus. Each child was holding a red or white or blue balloon and a Union Jack flag; for the new road was finished, and the Queen was coming to open it!

'Quick, quick,' she said as Clare and Ben and Rob ran in. 'Your balloons are in the hall. Mrs Dear has got them.'

They rushed into the school hall and there was Mrs Dear with three balloons, one of each colour, and three Union Jacks. Rob began at once telling her about the bear and the man walking on animals and sitting on them and Mrs Dear listened. She listened very hard. Then she told them why she thought the bear wouldn't squash people and how people could walk on animals, and the children listened and their eyes widened and widened.

'Oh,' said Clare, 'oh, *that's* how.'

'Are you ready, children?' called their mum. 'The bus is leaving.'

'Don't worry,' Mrs Dear called back, 'I'll bring Clare, Ben and Rob in my car. There's plenty of time. We won't be late.'

'But there *isn't* plenty of time, is there, Mrs Dear?' Clare whispered. 'Now we know that Mr Gunn is a big game hunter, and we know what he is *really* going to do with Steggie.'

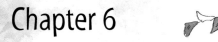

Chapter 6

What a morning it was, buzzing with
excitement. The new road was broad
and smooth with high banks on
either side. The men in hard hats,
the bulldozers and JCBs had gone,
and there, in the middle of the new
road was a platform with a red carpet
on it. Over the platform was an arch
with red, white and blue balloons
floating from it, and stretched across
the road in front of the platform was
a shining yellow ribbon.

The children from the little village school had a special place near the platform, because their Headteacher had been invited to sit on the platform.

'Look at the balloons and the ribbon!' said the children. 'And the Mayor with his gold chain. Oh, when will the Queen come?'

The waiting seemed to go on forever. Then, there was a cheer – the Queen had arrived. The Mayor welcomed her, the builder bowed.

Then the Mayor handed the Queen a pair of gold plated scissors and asked her to cut the ribbon and open the new road.

The Queen smiled and walked towards the yellow ribbon with the scissors in her hand.

But every head turned *away* from the Queen! Everyone was looking *down* the road! There was a huge gasp from the crowds lining the road. The Queen also stopped and looked up. Something huge was coming up the road. It was STEGGIE!

Clare, Ben, Rob and Mrs Dear quickly stepped out from the side of the road and stood in front of the Queen. Clare carried a red book, Ben and Rob carried a roll of paper, and Mrs Dear carried a very large, bulging plastic bag.

'Bow!' hissed Clare, and the boys bowed and she and Mrs Dear curtsied. Then Ben and Rob unrolled the paper and held it up. In large, rather wobbly black letters, it said,

Your Majesty
Please
save Steggie
from being
shot and
stuffed

Clare offered the book to the Queen. 'It's our school book about S-Steggie. It-it's got photographs and d-dates and everything, Y-Your Majesty.'

Mrs Dear dived into her bulging bag and brought out a huge piece of egg shell.

'Stegosaurus eggshell, Your Majesty, as hatched in our school library.'

The Queen looked at the notice, the children, the book, Mrs Dear and the eggshell, while Steggie walked steadily nearer. The Headteacher came swiftly down the steps, but the Mayor nipped in front of her.

'Your Majesty,' he gasped, 'please declare the road open. Steggie is about to be transported to an animal lover.'

'But he *doesn't* love them,' burst out Rob. 'He shoots them and stuffs them and he'll shoot and stuff Steggie.'

Steggie came closer. The crowd oohed and aahed. Rob turned and ran towards her. She stopped and touched him gently with her nose. She seemed to be trying to comfort him.

'Your Majesty, Your Majesty,' babbled the Mayor, '*please* cut the ribbon, and declare the road open.'

The Queen looked up at Steggie and down at the children, then she turned to the Mayor.

'Mr Mayor,' she said, 'do you know I am always opening things. It will be a change and a pleasure to close something.'

The Headteacher stepped up to the microphone and said, 'Everyone, pray silence for Her Majesty.'

The crowd hushed. Clare and Ben walked down to Steggie and stood on either side of her with their hands on her neck.

In a high, firm voice the Queen said, 'I declare this road…closed and I name it "STEGGIE'S WAY".'

And she didn't cut the ribbon.

'Close it both ends,' she commanded the builder, 'give her plenty of room.'

The builder stepped up to the Queen and bowed.

'I'll build another road, Your Majesty,' he promised, 'and keep all traffic well away from Steggie.'

'Hooray!' cheered the children. 'Hooray! Hooray! Hooray!'

When they got back to school, the Headteacher said, 'Well done, children! I am proud of you, and thank you, Mrs Dear, for helping.'

Then they sat down to a special 'Closing of the Road' tea party, and the Mayor and the governors came in afterwards and had some of the cake.

Later, the big game hunter got two letters. One was from the Manager of Flowery Meadows. It said,

Flowery Meadows
COUNTRY PARK

Dear Mr Gunn

Please remove your lorry from my park.
There is a big hole in the canvas and the ramp
is broken. I am getting complaints about it.

Yours sincerely,

M. Flowers

The other letter said,

2 Station Road
Littleton.
LB2 0NX

Dear Sir,

We got to Flowery Meadows
by sunrise and got Steggie into the
lorry, so we earned our five hundred
pounds each. You did not tell us that
she had four spikes on her tail and
that she does not sleep after meals.
We will not be working for you again.

Dick Brock (Driver)
Dennis Cott (Mate)

Chapter 7

The new road didn't remain smooth
for long. Grass began to grow out
from the edges, then flowers sprang
up in the grass. Bushes and saplings
grew on the steep banks where
Steggie couldn't go. Trees grew, taller
and taller, and the road became a
green glade full of flowers.

Clare, Ben and Rob were allowed to keep the yellow ribbon that the Queen hadn't cut and the Mayor and the Council kept the gold plated scissors that the Queen hadn't used. Mrs Dear kept one piece of egg shell and gave the rest to the Town Museum.

The big game hunter went off to Africa in a sulk to hunt more big game and was eaten by a lion when he wasn't looking. The lion was old and couldn't run after game as it used to, and its teeth were worn down, so it ate the hunter rather slowly.

And Steggie? Steggie got the best present of all – life.

Once a year the children of the village led by the Headteacher and Mrs Dear go down a secret path into the green glade to see Steggie.

They call it 'Steggie's Day' but they don't tell anyone, because they don't want any big game hunters to know they have a live dinosaur as a friend.

How did the children save Steggie?